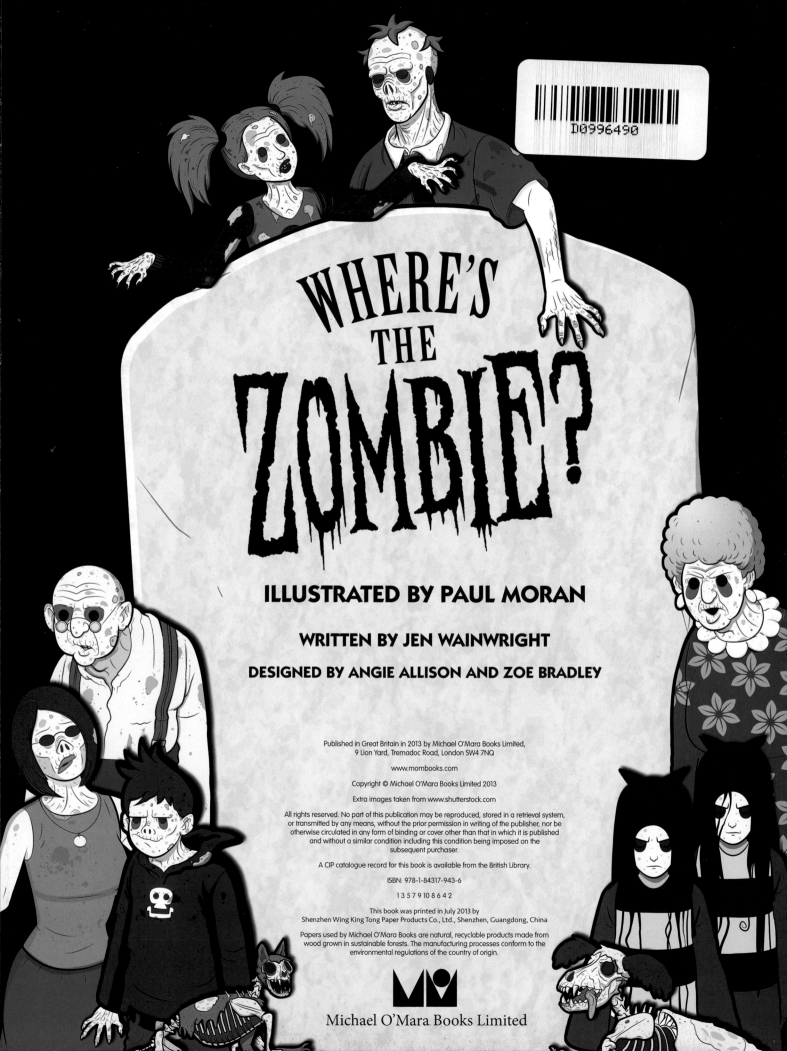

WHERE'S THE ZOMBIE?

ILLUSTRATED BY PAUL MORAN

WRITTEN BY JEN WAINWRIGHT

DESIGNED BY ANGIE ALLISON AND ZOE BRADLEY

Published in Great Britain in 2013 by Michael O'Mara Books Limited,
9 Lion Yard, Tremadoc Road, London SW4 7NQ

www.mombooks.com

Copyright © Michael O'Mara Books Limited 2013

Extra images taken from www.shutterstock.com

A CIP catalogue record for this book is available from the British Library.

ISBN: 978-1-84317-943-6

1 3 5 7 9 10 8 6 4 2

This book was printed in July 2013 by
Shenzhen Wing King Tong Paper Products Co., Ltd., Shenzhen, Guangdong, China

Papers used by Michael O'Mara Books are natural, recyclable products made from
wood grown in sustainable forests. The manufacturing processes conform to the
environmental regulations of the country of origin.

Michael O'Mara Books Limited

OUTBREAK AT LABORATORY

FEBRUARY 11th

Scientist Joel Peters is being held under quarantine after an accident at Hart Laboratories, upstate New York, last week.

Peters, 42, appears to have been exposed to a highly concentrated strain of a new virus, code named ZX-5, which he was developing at the lab.

NAME: J PETERS
EMPLOYEE NO: 24576
CLEARANCE LEVEL: 2

THE PETERS FAMILY AT A SUMMER BARBECUE LAST YEAR

Peters is described by his colleagues as a hardworking and reliable man. 'We don't understand how this happened,' said a source at the lab. 'His work is always so meticulous.'

He was removed from the home he shares with his elderly parents, wife Martha and four children on Saturday.

The exact nature of his symptoms is unclear, but doctors report a marked deterioration in his condition in the last 24 hours. His family was unavailable for comment.

PETERS FAMILY ON THE RUN

FEBRUARY 20th

Central News can reveal that Joel Peters has escaped from the secure quarantine unit where he was being held. It was confirmed yesterday that his family and pets are also infected with virus ZX-5. They have been reported missing.

Images of the Peters family have been released nationwide. Citizens are urged not to approach them under any circumstances.

'It is vital that the Peters family are located and safely contained,' said the head of Hart Laboratories last night.

'Please be on the lookout for them, and report any sightings to the police immediately. We urgently need to study them to understand more about how this extremely unpredictable virus operates.'

WARNING: DO NOT APPROACH THESE PEOPLE OR THESE ANIMALS. THEY ARE HIGHLY CONTAGIOUS AND EXTREMELY DANGEROUS.

Search for the ten members of the missing Peters family on every page. There are also ten medical kits to spot on each page to aid those thought to be infected.

BREAKING NEWS: March 3rd

City hospital quarantined after outbreak of new virus.

Baffled doctors describe victims as 'walking dead'.

Have you seen this family?

LIVE

BREAKING NEWS: March 8th

Officials concerned virus may be airborne.

Citizens strongly advised to avoid crowded public spaces.

Have you seen this family?

LIVE

BREAKING NEWS: March 17th

Infection is spreading at speed in urban areas.

Officials now classifying the virus as a Level 1 epidemic.

Have you seen this family?

BREAKING NEWS: March 22nd

Schools across the region to close.

Ringhill High remaining open despite fears.

Have you seen this family?

LIVE

BREAKING NEWS: March 30th

Families transform subway station into bunker.

Panic sets in as number of infected victims keeps rising.

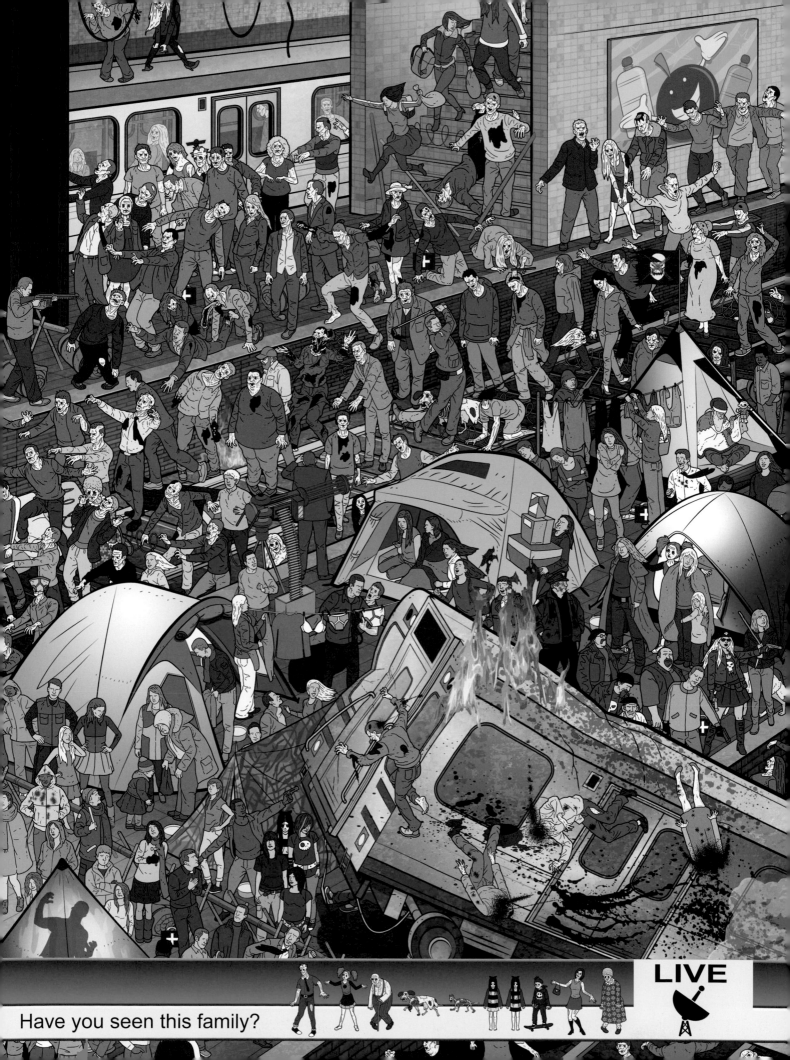

Have you seen this family?

BREAKING NEWS: March 31st

Looters target city's banking district.

Armed thieves ignore high risk of contamination from infected 'zombies'.

Have you seen this family?

LIVE

BREAKING NEWS: April 4th

Confirmed zombie sightings outside urban exclusion zones.

Crisis talks are being held as containment efforts fail.

Have you seen this family?

LIVE

BREAKING NEWS: April 10th

White House overrun.

President evacuated to safe house in the face of zombie riots.

Have you seen this family?

BREAKING NEWS: May 5th

Underground evacuation plan aborted.

Zombies attack Silvertown sewers, blocking planned escape route.

Have you seen this family?

LIVE

BREAKING NEWS: May 15th

Fortress Z falls …

Answers

BREAKING NEWS: March 3rd

City hospital quarantined after outbreak of new virus.

Baffled doctors describe victims as 'walking dead'   Have you seen this family?   LIVE

BREAKING NEWS: March 8th

Officials concerned virus may be airborne.

Citizens strongly advised to avoid crowded public spaces.   Have you seen this family?   LIVE

BREAKING NEWS: March 17th

Infection is spreading at speed in urban areas.

Officials now classifying the virus as a Level 1 epidemic.

Have you seen this family?

LIVE

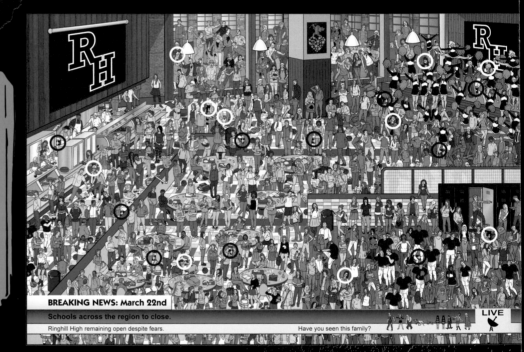

BREAKING NEWS: March 22nd

Schools across the region to close.

Ringhill High remaining open despite fears.

Have you seen this family?

LIVE

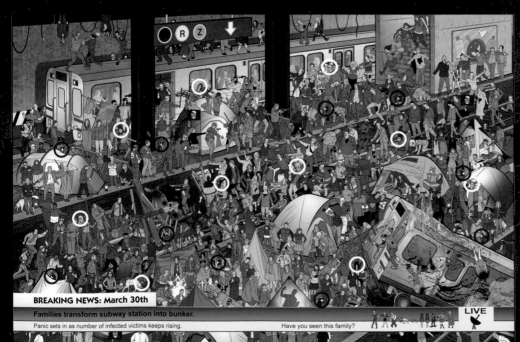

BREAKING NEWS: March 30th

Families transform subway station into bunker.

Panic sets in as number of infected victims keeps rising.

Have you seen this family?

LIVE

BREAKING NEWS: March 31st

Looters target city's banking district.

Armed thieves ignore high risk of contamination from infected 'zombies'.　Have you seen this family?　LIVE

Extra Spots

A graffiti artist ☐

Zombies on leashes ☐

A guy kicking down a door ☐

A head shot from a motorcycle ☐

Weightlifting with a zombie ☐

Extra Spots

man rising from the dead ☐

cow decapitating someone ☐

lucky shot through the roof ☐

lasso ☐

cow being sawn in half ☐

BREAKING NEWS: April 4th

Confirmed zombie sightings outside urban exclusion zone.

Crisis talks are being held as containment efforts fail.　Have you seen this family?　LIVE

BREAKING NEWS: April 10th

White House overrun.

President evacuated to safe house in the face of zombie riots.　Have you seen this family?　LIVE

Extra Spots

Extreme photocopying ☐

Two kids hiding ☐

A zombie giving a headlock ☐

Two vases of flowers ☐

A zombie maid ☐

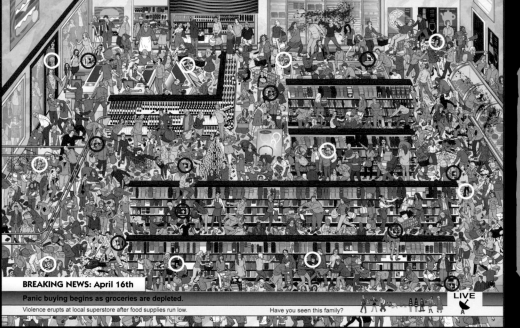

BREAKING NEWS: April 16th
Panic buying begins as groceries are depleted.
Violence erupts at local superstore after food supplies run low.   Have you seen this family?
LIVE

BREAKING NEWS: April 22nd
Chaos on the roads.
Survivors head for ports in huge numbers.   Have you seen this family?
LIVE

BREAKING NEWS: April 28th
Saharan plane crash tragedy.
All crash survivors confirmed as infected.   Have you seen this family?
LIVE